Alone

AMY LAURENS

Alone

INKLET #17

AMY LAURENS

Inkprint PRESS

www.inkprintpress.com

Print ISBN: 978-1-925825-16-9
eBook ISBN: 9781386403883

www.inkprintpress.com

*National Library of Australia Cataloguing-in-Publication
Data*
Laurens, Amy 1985 –
Alone
46 p.
ISBN: 978-1-925825-16-9
Inkprint Press, Canberra, Australia
1. Fiction—Fantasy—General 2. Fiction—Short
Stories

First Print Edition: September 2019
Cover design © Inkprint Press
Interior art © Amy Laurens

ALONE

H E LINGERS OVER HIS APPROACH TO the front door, breathing deeply, filling his dry, creaky lungs with the scent of home. Stone and damp, old tomatoes and dust. His life encapsulated by a perfect smell.

And he'll never smell it again. The soulbond is drawing to an end, he can feel it, feel the weight lifting. Two days, he estimates. Two days and the bond will be gone. He'll be alone for the first time in years.

He casts his gaze over the two storeys of the little house, crammed in at the end of a high-walled alleyway—and yet the only place he's ever been able to breathe. The gang—his family, the ones he chose and raised—are like that. They kept him going when there was nothing else to live for.

He winces. What is he thinking? They need him, his protection—and he needs them. He pauses stiffly on the front step, rubbing the age from his knuckles and the pain from his face.

He opens the door and Tara storms out into the hall. She attacks the stairs without even a glance in his direction. His mouth bunches tightly as he suppresses a laugh. Oh, yes. This is home.

He steps inside and closes the door behind him, smoothing a hand over wood more worn than he is. He takes another deep breath, basking in the warm smells of oak and brass polish.

A sigh, from the living room. Is that her? Fortuitous, if so. The more of them he can avoid today the better. Dying is hard enough without having to say goodbye.

Especially when one must die alone.

He creeps across the hallway, floor-boards gently protesting, and pauses for a moment in the doorway to drink in the scene. The bay window to his left lets in the little light available in this bottom storey of a back alley, softly illuminating the furniture older than he is—and probably in better condition. His lips twitch in a half smile.

And there, curled in the single armchair by the fireplace, bathed in flickering firelight, sits Jessana. He smiles at the contradiction of the literary novel in her hand and the assassin's knife lying on the table next to her, loving it even as he hates himself for nurturing the killer in her. But it had been necessary, a choice of her life, the life of his almost-daughter, against the lives of faceless, imper-sonal others. He'd kept her alive by teaching her his skills.

He tenses, thinking of what he is about to do; it feels precariously like abandoning her. Pain stabs at his ribcage. He sucks in air that tastes like age and smooths the mask over his face. They will never know about the pain—but the goodbye he can't delay much longer. So he straightens from the wall, squares his shoulders, and enters the room.

Jess glances up and smiles. "Hello!" She unfurls her legs to get to her feet, but he waves her back down.

"No need for that." He lowers himself into a nearby chair and nods at her clenched fist. "What have you got there?"

Jess sighs and rolls her eyes, putting down her book and offering her other hand. "Tara found it."

"Unusual." The glossy black ring seems the antithesis of Jess, shrouded in darkness as she is haloed in light. For a moment he feels as though it tugs at his soulbond; but the moment passes, and it is just a ring, if an unusually deep black one.

"Very," Jess responds. "And I don't even want to know where she got it from, especially if it's where I think she did."

"And where might that be?"

"A dead body."

"Oh, Jess," he says, laughing. "You've got your hands full with that one." He grins; Jess grins back.

"Is there any hope?" she asks in mock despair.

He sobers. "Funny you should say that," he murmurs. "I was just thinking the other day that she reminded me of someone." He shoots Jess a significant look.

She responds with a wry smile. "Okay," she says. "I give in. I'll persevere with the little monster."

He chuckles. "Good girl."

The silence stretches.

Jess glances at her novel, then back at him. "Did you want something?"

It's time. It has to be done. His mind races for things to say, anything other than what needs to be said.

Nothing comes, so he inhales and begins. "Yes, Jessana, I do want something."

Her body language changes, becoming more alert. "Is everything all right?"

He smiles. "Everything is fine. In... in a manner of speaking. You see, it appears that I have..." He swallows, almost choking on the lie. "I have a son."

Jess jerks in surprise.

"Yes," he continues, finding his rhythm. "I was somewhat shocked myself to discover it. But the main point is, he is quite unwell, and his mother is unable to support them with all his medical expenses." A slight pause before the climax of the lie. "I loved his mother very much. I... I have found a job." He stares at the floor, sick to the stomach. "I'm going to live with them, and support them."

He risks a glance at Jess, whose shock is written on her face. Shock, but not disbelief. That's a good sign.

He presses on, the hardest part behind him. "The house will need a new leader, Jessana. I want that leader to be you."

"Me?" she says, incredulous. "Why me? There are others much better qualified. River is the eldest, choose him! Or Patty, she knows how to get everyone moving. Or Alek, or..." She flounders. "Why me?"

He smiles gently. "It has always been you, Jessana. From the moment you arrived. Don't you notice how they follow you?"

The whole world worships the ground you walk on, he doesn't add.

Jess squirms. "I suppose so..."

He takes her hand. "They will support you. Never alone, remember? Do it for me?" He blinks back the tears that threaten to clog his eyes. Their motto, everything they live by—but he has to throw it away. He can't cling to false hope, can't risk having the bond transfer to someone he loves when he passes on.

Jess nods, exhaling. "Okay," she says. "For you."

"Then good." He claps his hands once together and smiles. "That's settled." He makes to rise.

"When do you leave?" Jess says softly, and he feels her eyes probing his facade for the truth, pinning him back in his chair.

He shakes off her gaze, stands and closes his eyes; turns away from love and comfort and joy.

"It's today, isn't it?" she says.

He nods.

"Oh."

And she is there, beside him, wrapping her arms around him, and the tears that he'd promised he wouldn't shed are coursing down his cheeks, making rivulets to rival his wrinkles.

Slowly, her soothing works its way into the crevices of his soul and the tears subside like dust settling to the ground. Jess pats him on the shoulder. "You should go, then," she says. "Wouldn't want to be late, now, would we?"

He smiles, a false, brittle thing that he erases before it cracks his fragile exterior. He flees to the front door and jerks it open, determined not to look back. He steps out, pulls the door—but Jess catches it and props it open, standing to watch him leave.

He walks away down the alley. Midway, Jess calls. "Wait!"

He steels himself, knowing he can't deny her the chance for goodbye. He tenses as he meets her gaze, so piercing he thinks it might kill him there and then.

"Wait," she says again.

"Yes, Jessana?"

"How much longer do you have to live?"

And there it is, the very thing he's been trying to avoid, the reason he'd concocted the story of the job and the family in the first place. And despite it all, in spite of all his acting and plotting and planning—she knows. She still knows.

He works his tongue to moisten his suddenly dry mouth. "Not... Not much longer," he says in a voice that rasps like dead leaves.

"How long?"

Those eyes. Stars of Fate, those eyes... He presses his own closed and forces the words out. "Two days."

The silence and curiosity opens his eyes. Their gazes lock, and she nods. "Two days. Stay nearby. I'll find you."

"You can't!" he says, hands clenching. "I won't have the bond jump to you!"

Jess smiles sadly. "It can't. I'm already bound."

He reels like she's slammed the door in his face. Jess, his precious, perfect Jess, is soulbound too. No wonder she'd seen through his lies.

He nods. "Nearby." She deserves that much. He turns to leave.

"Wait."

Something thuds into the ground behind his feet, and he glances down. Her knife. His gaze flicks to Jess.

"For the pain," she says.

He nods and picks up the knife. "For the pain." Tucking it into his belt, he walks out of the alleyway for the last time.

Behind him, words echo down the street that smells like home. "Never alone, Guiro. Never alone."

THE MAKING OF
ALONE

Like the very first Inklet, *Another Kind Of Hunger*, this story was written as I specifically tried to flesh out some character development for a novel I was working on. The novel, *Jesscapades*, was the second novel I ever wrote, about secret assassins and fate and learning about corruption in what basically amounts to your religion.

It was—still is—a super fun book, both to write, and later, for me to go back and read. But the middle of it's a hot mess.

Put it this way: in the intervening years, that one single novel has been teased out into its separate strands and become at least four different novels, some of which you'll get to see one day. (At the bare minimum, I'm committed to writing one with the title *Jesscapades*, because in 2018 I found a pre-made cover that I fell in love with and had made up with the most-original version of *Jesscapades* in mind.)

Alone was one of my many, many attempts to detangle all those plot threads—to motivate some of the apparently random story decisions I'd made, and to try to reconcile some of the conflicting information about the main character that had spawned in this detangling process.

The main character of the original novel is Jess, only the novel occurs after [redacted] dies and Jess is estranged from the house, only I needed a reason for…

Look, it's complicated, okay? And this was just one of many, many attempts to make it all make sense.

And honestly? I'm not sure it helped that much at all :'D

Oh well. At least I got a story.

DOWNLOAD YOUR FREE EBOOK

When you buy a print book from Inkprint Press, we like to say THANK YOU by offering you the ebook for free!

Please head to
www.inkprintpress.com/inklets/17/
and the use the coupon 17INK to get your copy of this Inklet in epub AND mobi today!
(Coupon will only work once.)

Read more by Amy Laurens!

WHERE SHADOWS RISE

CHAPTER ONE

THE DOORBELL RANG. That doesn't sound exciting in and of itself, but let me assure you: it was the most heart-pounding thing to happen all week. It was my birthday, I was home alone, and because of the stupid witness protection business, I'd been stuck in the house all summer. I hadn't even been allowed out to see friends, because we'd arrived in town at the end of last year with only three school weeks to go—so I didn't have any friends.

Well. I had friends, but they were back in Melbourne, and I wasn't allowed to contact them for fear someone would track down our new location. Lucky me.

Anyway, it was my birthday, I was alone because Mum and Dad had gone to do something regarding birthday surprises and Anna had inexplicably chosen to go with them, and the door-bell had just rung. I stared at the closed door, heart pounding, while our chocolate Labrador, Veve, tried to chew it down. Was I going to open it?

Of course I was going to open it. The chances of it being a mobster were slim to none; for starters, a mobster wouldn't have rung the bell.

I opened it.

"Miss Tanning?" The deliveryman raised a questioning eyebrow and cocked a digital pen at me.

I nodded, heart flip-flopping, and scrawled a fair impersonation of my signature on the digital pad.

He handed over a small, brown-paper parcel with a handwritten address, and departed.

I closed the door behind him, throat dry, and stared down at Veve. On the one hand, yay birthday present. On the other, holy crap, someone had our address. That was *not* a good thing.

It became even less of a good thing when I noticed that the parcel was indeed addressed to a Miss Tanning: a Miss *Anna* Tanning, as in my sister, not me, Emma Tanning.

Anger bubbled up in my chest, hot and tight, and the parcel protested in my grip.

Veve whined softly.

"How could she *do* this?" I whispered to Veve.

I turned the parcel over. It was from Kade, Anna's frogging ex-boyfriend. Who apparently wasn't an 'ex' after all.

Urgh. I ground my teeth. "You know what?" I asked Veve.

She looked up at me with her liquid brown eyes, tongue lolling as she smiled.

"Screw it. If Anna can get interstate mail from people who aren't even supposed to know we exist anymore, you and I can go for a walk on my birthday. What do you think?"

They say dogs don't speak English, but Veve sure as heck knew the word 'walk'—though I think in her vocabulary it was something closer to 'Magical Trip To Disneyland' and less like 'Comparatively Bland Meander Through Trees'.

She tucked her tail right under her butt and shot down the hall, whirling in frantic circles a few times at the end before pelting back as I retrieved her lead from the drawer in the front cabinet.

I rolled my eyes as I clipped her lead onto her collar. For my troubles, I got slimed right up the nostrils. "You're disgusting, you know that?" I wiped off the worst of the dog slobber on the shoulder of my shirt. She just grinned.

Out on the street, she leapt and twisted madly. "Hair-brain," I told her, snapping the lead to get her attention. "It's just a walk."

She just snorted—and stiffened. I followed her gaze to where a flock of corellas pecked their way through the dry grass at the end of the street.

"Veve!"

My shout was in vain: the lead burned through my fingers and Veve shot down the road, a chocolate bullet howling death and destruction for all things feathered.

I cursed her to the lower circles of doggie hell. Which probably involved, I don't know, a world devoid of birds, cats, people, sunshine, and walks, if Veve was anything to go by.

"Veve!" If the sight of the mad Lab-rat barrelling toward them hadn't scared the birds off, my shouts would have. "Come back here *now!*"

Predictably, she ignored me, pounding down the slope, through the fringe of gum trees, and down the narrow stairs between giant granite boulders that led to the river.

"Stupid frogging brainless beast of a stupid frogging dog," I muttered as I followed. "If Mum gets home before we do and freaks out, I swear, I'll pluck your tail hairs out."

Empty threats, obviously, but Mum's freak-out wouldn't be. Her thoughts would go straight to the day Anna nearly died—and I wouldn't blame her.

I should have left a note. Urgh.

The stairs ended and I found myself on a track broad enough for two twisting along a creek the colour of bitter tea. Tussock grass clustered in spikes—where the eucalypts would let it—and hot summer sunlight glinted from the leaves. Somewhere to my right, downstream and in the opposite direction to the house, Veve barked. I exhaled like a whale coming up for air and set out after her.

Veve bounded out from the under-growth in front of me, a dolphin leaping through water, tongue flapping with every bound. "Stupid mutt," I told her under my breath.

She didn't care what I thought (of course), and saved a leap for the last minute so she could plant muddy feet on my hips as I tried to catch her collar.

I straightened, about to insult her some more, and realised that she'd gone stiff again, ears pricked and mouth tight, listening down the path.

My neck prickled. Someone was coming. A second later, I heard foot-steps in the gravel, and a low, male voice, humming, or maybe singing softly.

My chest constricted, and just as suddenly my hands were slick. Chan-ces were it was just a stranger out for a midday stroll, but my stomach wound knots about my memories and

I smelled the hot concrete and melting asphalt, old oil and stale urine of the Lilydale train station where the body had been hidden in a toilet stall, the body of the girl who'd looked like Anna.

I had to get off the path.

"Come on, Veve," I said, pulling her close, white-knuckled as I stepped into the undergrowth. The tea tree scrub protested, but I shoved my way through anyway, glancing over my shoulder as the humming grew louder.

I kept going until I couldn't hear footsteps any more, until the wind swallowed the hum that sounded too like the warning cry of a hive—danger, we're working here, come close and get stung. I didn't want to get stung; visions of a blood-streaked face refused to be blinked away.

Only Veve tugging brought me back to myself, and I realised firstly that I was holding the lead way too tight, cutting off Veve's air supply, secondly that the reason my cheeks were suddenly cold was because I'd been crying, and thirdly that I'd found the creek again, looping back parallel maybe fifty meters or so from the path.

Abruptly, I dropped Veve's lead and strode forward to kneel by the water. I dipped my hands in. A shiver slid through me at its chill, and I scooped it up to wash my face.

Flinging the excess water away, I gulped at the air, deep, calming breaths all the way down into my belly, and visualised a river washing away the blood from my thoughts, just like the police psych had taught me.

Once the space behind my eyes was calm and black, I drew in one last forceful breath, and opened my eyes. Perched on a rock by the creek, I hugged my knees to my chest as cool water lapped at my toes. Veve was a little upstream, just before the creek bent back toward the path, doggy paddling in circles in a deep spot where the water broadened to maybe ten meters across. In front of me it was broad but shallow, only ankle deep, its path torn to white foam by the rocks.

And—I gasped. In the middle of the stream, glittering in the sun like a piece of fallen sky, was the hugest butterfly I'd ever seen.

Which was pretty huge; besides the fact that I grew up visiting the Melbourne Zoo with its impressive butterfly house every Christmas since I could remember, Mum and Dad had taken us up to Brisbane for a family holiday two years ago, and we'd seen giant tropical butterflies bigger than my hand.

This one, bright blue with black edging like a Ulysses, was bigger than both my hands put together.

And then it turned around.

Okay. I'd grown up reading fairy tales as much as the next person, and although I'd had a horse-crazy stage instead of a fairy-crazy stage like Anna had, I'd seen all her paraphernalia.

Still, none of it prepared me for finding something that looked exactly like a fairy, standing smack in the middle of a creek in boring, back-water Nowra.

I'm pretty sure my eyes were only hanging in their sockets by a thread.

And then it talked.

Her face lit up like a cloud had just uncovered the sun as she spotted me. "Hi there!" she said, fluttering over.

I just stared, heart pounding against my ribcage as though it wanted to run away from the absurdity of it all. "No," I said. "I'm hallucinating."

The fairy frowned. "I don't think so."

I shook my head. "No. No, things like this do not happen. Things like this aren't *real*." I stood, backing up a step.

The fairy sighed. "I promise. I'm quite real."

"You would say that, wouldn't you," I said, eyeing her. "Veve!" I waved at the dog and hopped from one foot to the other, trying to lure her in with the promise of play. "We're going now!"

Veve, adorable beast that she was, landed a little upstream and shook vigorously before trotting toward me. I backed hurriedly away from the bank, dancing to keep Veve's attention.

"Wait!" the fairy cried, wings snapping out and propelling her a couple of feet into the air. "You're a Traveller! I need to talk to you!"

"Uh huh, sure," I said as I wound the lead around my hand and set off back into the bushes. This was punishment for leaving the house, obviously. The universe was out to get me, reminding me forcefully that once you started disregarding some rules, who knew what other rules you'd end up flouting.

The rules of physics, for example.

I glanced back once, right before the bushes hid the stream altogether. Blue flashed, high up, but I ducked to get a better view and it was only the sky. I scowled. Stupid fairy. Stupid universe. Served me right for leaving the house in the first place. Urgh. "Come on, Veve," I said, snapping the lead. "Even if the house is prison, at least it's *sane*."

I was stomping so furiously as I burst out onto the path that when a figure rose from a stoop only a couple of steps away, I squeaked in surprise.

I scowled. People rarely surprised me; usually I could tell without trying that someone was near. I really must have been off in my own little world.

I glowered at the boy who lived to make my school life a misery. "What are you doing here?" I snapped. "Isn't it bad enough that I have to deal with you on school days? Which, by the way, don't start until tomorrow. You're ruining my holidays."

Okay, so maybe that was a little harsh, but come on. It was *Scott*. I'd arrived in town with three weeks left in the school year, and he'd spent every day of them humiliating me in front of his mates, and I didn't care for a repeat this year.

Scott eyed me warily, which was a strange expression on him.

Usually he strode around like he knew without a doubt that he was too good for the world, and also—somewhere deeper, somewhere I'd only caught a glimpse of once or twice— that it had nothing left to throw at him that could hurt.

Occasionally, in my more generous moments, I wondered what had happened to make him look that way.

Mostly, however, I just wondered why he was such a moron.

"What are you doing here?" he asked, voice dripping with accusation and suspicion.

My hands fisted of their own accord, and beside me Veve's hackles rose as she chimed in with a low-pitched, rumbling growl. I flicked the free end of the lead at her nose. "Nothing," I said, in a rousing blaze of wit. "What are you doing?"

He scowled. "You shouldn't be here."

For one heart-stopping instant I thought he meant out here generally, walking around, as if he knew what had happened and why I'd hidden away all summer. Then I realised he was nodding into the undergrowth. I rolled my eyes. "I might be a city slicker," I bit off, "but I'm not stupid. I made enough noise to scare off a herd of elephants, let alone any snakes that might have been lying around." The thought chilled me, though; I *hadn't* been thinking about snakes when I'd hurried off the path. One badly-timed footstep and a brown snake bite later, and I could be a dead body too.

But Scott had moved on, stalking off down the path. He had nice shoulders, I'd give him that much. Pity he couldn't derive his personality from them, instead of whatever dead weight it was he kept inside his head for brains.

Beside me, Veve growled again, louder this time, more urgent. I snapped the lead at her and stared after Scott's retreating form, trying to think of something cutting.

It was only when Veve growled for the third time that I realised she wasn't even facing Scott. Instead, she was looking back into the bushes—and something dark was flickering in there, deep in the shadows of the trees.

My chest squeezed in on itself and adrenalin shot through my body. Veve's growling grew louder until it broke in a bark, something midway between slavering and terrified, and I realised my tongue was stuck to the roof of my mouth. Carefully I peeled it away, unable to tear my eyes from the shifting darkness in the bushes. There was no discernible form, just shadow, darker than it should have been this soon after midday, and a pervasive sense of dread clamping down on me like an on-coming storm.

Veve began backing away, hackles prickling, growl rising and falling like thunder. I glanced down at her, back to the shadows—and they were closer, much closer than they had been.

I turned and bolted.

Keep reading! Head to
http://www.amylaurens.com/book
s/sanctuary/where-shadows-rise/
to buy your copy now!

ABOUT THE AUTHOR

AMY LAURENS is an Australian author of fantasy fiction for all ages. In addition to the *Sanctuary* series of portal fantasy stories set in Nowra, Australia, Amy has written the humorous fantasy series *Kaditeos: Mercury*, beginning with *How Not To Acquire A Castle*, as well as a whole bunch of non-fiction for writers and non-writers alike.

Jesscapades and its various incarnations will join this list someday. You'll recognise them, because they'll all be about secret assassins.

You can find out more about Amy at her website, www.amylaurens.com.

INKLETS

Collect them all! Released on the 1st and 15th of each month.

INKLET #007
SEVENTY
LIANA BROOKS

INKLET #008
A Final Request
for Mercy
AMY LAURENS

INKLET #009
the kitten psychologist
VS.
the kitten's owners
THEA VAN DIEPEN

INKLET #010
Answer the
Question
AMY LAURENS

INKLET #011
Happily,
Red
AMY LAURENS

INKLET #012
the kitten psychologist
tries to be patient
through email
THEA VAN DIEPEN

INKLET #013
DRAGON
Tuesday
AMY LAURENS

INKLET #014
RED PLANET
REFUGEES
LIANA BROOKS

INKLET #015
the kitten psychologist &
What The Kitten Did
THEA VAN DIEPEN

Cherry Blossom
AMY LAURENS
Alone
AMY LAURENS
the kitten psychologist & The Kitten Come To A Conclusion
THEA VAN DIEPEN
LEVEL NINE
LIANA BROOKS
To Dust
AMY LAURENS
Interchange
AMY LAURENS
Emalia's Lanterns
LIANA BROOKS
Dear Santa
AMY LAURENS
The Quilt-Maker's Scrap
AMY L. LAURENS